CEASE TO WEEP

By Simon Trowbridge

FICTION

Élodie Duquette

NON-FICTION

Aix: A History of the Aix-en-Provence Festival

The Music of Bruce Springsteen and the E Street Band

The Rise and Fall of the Royal Shakespeare Company: An
Illustrated History

The Comédie-Française from Molière to Éric Ruf

Rameau

The Company

CEASE TO WEEP

Novella

Followed by Four Stories

SIMON TROWBRIDGE

Englance *Press*

First published in 2023
by Englance Press, Oxford

ISBN 978-1-7384215-2-7

'The Encore' was first published in
Shenandoah in 2014 (vol.64, n.1)

Life has got to be allowed to continue even after the dream of life is-all-over.

TENNESSEE WILLIAMS

Contents

Cease to Weep
Novella

Oft have I heard that grief softens the mind,
And makes it fearful and degenerate;
Think therefore on revenge and cease to weep.

SHAKESPEARE

South Oxfordshire

The lunatic asylum was empty and derelict. There was a persistent stench of silage. At the start of the village, I turned off the main road and followed a country lane that climbed across the muddy acres of a pig farm towards the white sky. Corrugated iron shelters and barrels of pink meat had replaced most of the cornfields. And yet it was the smell of corn in the dust that took me back years – I could not escape the fact that I was home.

I knew every corner of the road so when I reached a point that gave a view, back down into the valley, of the village and the hills on the other side of the river, I slowed almost to a halt. The wrought iron gates appeared suddenly, on the other side of the lane, half-hidden by trees. They were badly rusted but the 'Keep Out' sign had been freshly painted. The drive was a dirt track, a long tunnel through the wood. The house, when it finally appeared, looked unchanged. I pulled to a halt on the gravel forecourt and stepped from the car. The tall double doors were open. I pressed the bell and turned to swipe the dust from my black trousers. A figure approached from across the dark hall, a young woman of around twenty. Her eyes were sleepy and a little sullen. She lifted her arms to tie back her dishevelled hair.

'Mrs Root's not here,' she said. 'If you're involved in the arrangements please go round the side.' She yawned.

I smiled. 'Do I look like a caterer?'

'Oh.'

'I'm Joseph, Mrs Root's son.'

'They're still at the church.'

'Can I come in?'

I followed her into the house and along a corridor. She took me into a long white room, sparsely furnished, with a wall of open French windows. There was a swimming pool, a marquee, and a wide expanse of lawn. Waitresses in formal black were setting tables for the wake. The heatwave had scorched the land. The pool was deliciously incongruous in this landscape of ruined grass. The girl was leaving. 'Stay and talk to me for a while.'

She sat on a long couch. I sat at the other end. 'So, who are you?'

She leant forward and stroked her shin. 'Do you mind if I smoke?'

'No.'

She took out a cigarette and then offered the packet. 'Do you?'

'Yes, but I won't.'

She lit the cigarette. 'She doesn't like me to smoke in the house.' She took a drag, watching me.

'What's your name?'

'Rachel.'

'What do you do?'

'I was working for your father.'

'Stepfather. As what?'

'Research assistant.'

'You're a student?'

'Ah hah. Mrs Root didn't tell me you were coming.'

'No.'

'I really ought to get on.'

'I'd like to rest for a while. Can you show me where?'

We went up two flights to the second floor. She reached for a door. I touched her arm. 'No.' I walked down the corridor to a door at the end. 'This one.' We entered a dark room. I released the blinds, and the space took light like the flash of a camera. There were yellow walls, empty bookcases, and a bed. The windows looked out on the garden and the downs beyond. The floorboards were bare. A membrane of dust covered the surfaces.

'This room isn't used,' she said.

'It used to be my room.'

'Can I go now?'

'Can you fetch me a black tie?'

'Where from?'

She walked away. I was tired, in need of rest. I must have slept for a couple of hours. Downstairs, the wake was in full swing. I wandered between the groups of people. There was a look in my mother's eyes I'd never seen before, although she was going through the motions with her usual grace. I kissed her on the cheek, and she smiled. 'Where were you?'

'I was in Berlin. I drove all night.'

'We'll talk later,' she said.

A hand squeezed my shoulder. I turned to see my stepbrother.

'I'm glad you came,' Gerald said.

I hadn't seen him for nearly three years. His cold, light-blue eyes were the same, but he had become thickset, and what was left of his hair was cut close to his temples. He looked like his father. A beautiful young woman held his hand. She wore spectacles and her brown hair was tied up.

'We tried to contact you.'

'I haven't been reading emails. I only found out when I saw an English paper yesterday.'

'What were you doing in Berlin?'

'Working.'

He paused. 'Well, at least you're here. It's been too long. This is Judith.' We shook hands.

Later, I broke away and walked to the edge of the garden, through the orchard to where the lawn gave way to scrubland and open country. The house and its downland estate had been in my mother's family for generations. It had been temporarily annexed by my stepfather, her keeper; he had rationed her love. I intended to reclaim my mother and this country. I walked on, following a path that climbed to the top of the hill.

When I returned to the house, it was twilight. Gerald and Judith were sitting in the long room, silent and apart. 'Where's Mother?' I asked

'She's gone to bed,' Judith said. 'She was upset. She thought you'd left.'

Gerald said, 'You haven't been here for years. The day we bury him you turn up.'

I sat down on the couch beside Judith. She was my age, years younger than Gerald. 'You can't intimidate me anymore,' I told him.

'I just want us to be friends.' He started to ask questions about my recent life. 'What was the job in Berlin?'

'Writing music for a TV serial.'

'Judith's an actress,' he said.

'I've just left drama school,' she said.

Out in the garden, a match flared. Gerald went to

the open windows. 'Who's there? Come here.' He returned to his chair. 'That girl's still here,' he told Judith.

Rachel appeared at the window.

'Why are you still here?' Gerald said.

'Your mother didn't say I should go.'

'Your work has finished.'

'That isn't true.'

'No, I want you to leave his work alone. I want you to leave this house.'

'Right now?'

'In the morning. First thing.'

'If your mother says so.'

He stared at her.

'Can I go now?'

She retreated into the darkness.

The next morning, I joined my mother for breakfast. Gerald and Judith and already left for London.

Mother's fair hair was cut fashionably short; she was wearing black trousers and a white blouse and looked much younger than her age. She poured coffee. I waited to feel something. if not love, then an approximation of love.

'All these years you haven't come here,' Mother said. 'It hurts me that you waited for Robin's death to come.'

'Have you forgotten how your husband and his son treated me?'

'Robin tried so hard with you. I think we shouldn't talk about it. I'm just glad that you're here.'

After breakfast I went into the study. The desk drawers and filing cabinet were unlocked but empty of papers. On the mantelpiece there were some photographs, among them a family snapshot that must have been taken shortly after my mother's second marriage. I looked at my nine-year-old self scowling at the camera, surrounded by the taller, smiling faces of Mother, Robin, and Gerald.

Somers Town, later that day

I parked beneath a large mural depicting Dickensian St Pancras, opposite a terrace of old, yellow-brick, houses. A middle-aged skinhead followed two pit bulls down the street. A girl was sitting on the steps outside my house. It was Rachel.

'What are you doing here?'

'Waiting for you.'

'How did you know where to find me?'

'I looked in your mother's address book. It's not private, it's beside her phone. She did what your brother wanted. Told me to leave.'

'What do you want from me?'

'I want to complete the work I was doing for your father.'

'Stepfather.'

We went inside. The hall was littered with mail. She wandered around the almost empty rooms, too on edge to stay still. When my girlfriend moved out, last winter, she took with her most of the furniture, but I had bought a couch and a TV set, which I now switched on so that we could avoid small talk. I went into the kitchen to make coffee and Rachel followed. 'Stay and watch TV,' I said. 'We'll talk in a minute.'

'Can I have a drink?'

She leant against the sink, raised one knee, and waited. Back in the living room, she sat on the floor, close to the TV set, like a child. I handed her a vodka. A tennis match was being shown, and she watched the play intently, silently, and I thought to myself, what does this mean? At length I said, 'What exactly do you want me to do?'

'He took the PC, disks and papers, everything I was working on with Robin. The book's almost complete, I want to prepare it for publication.'

'And you want me to get them back?'

'Yes. Can you do that?'

'Maybe. Why didn't you go to the funeral?'

'I couldn't face it.'

'You were fond of him?'

'Yes. I'm sorry, I'm not feeling well, where's the toilet?'

I told her and she rushed out. I heard her vomiting. When she came back her face was colourless.

'I've had too much to drink.'

'One vodka?'

'I came from the pub. I don't normally drink. A friend's birthday.'

For several hours she couldn't stop vomiting. I gave her the bed and tried to sleep on the couch.

Sometime later she came quietly into the room. She felt her way in the darkness, switched on the kitchen light and closed the door. I heard her pour herself a glass of water. The door opened. She could see that I was awake

'I didn't mean to wake you.'

'I wasn't asleep.'

'A girl left some clothes. I borrowed a T-shirt. Is that okay?'

'It's fine. Keep it.'

She left a pause. 'Why don't we share the bed? I mean, if you want to.'

'I'm okay. You're not well. Go back to bed.'

I woke to find that I was lying on the floor. It was almost morning. I went into the bedroom and climbed carefully into the bed. When the alarm woke us, she was lying against my chest. Embarrassed, we separated.

'I'll see what I can do about your work,' I said.

'Thank you.' She gave me her number.

Chelsea, Hampstead and Somers Town

Three days after the funeral, Gerald sent an email inviting me to his home. I parked near Sloane Square and walked down a street of large houses with stucco facades. I met Judith at the door. 'Gerald's probably in his study. Tell him I'm taking a bath, will you?' She ran up the stairs.

I found Gerald in the living room, watching cricket. He stood up and shook my hand, then slapped me on the back. 'Scotch?' He poured the drinks. 'I wanted to apologise.'

We watched the match for a while.

'This is good,' Gerald said. 'We haven't shared a drink for a long time.'

I could remember Gerald beating me up; Gerald teasing me with his girlfriends; but sharing a dram on a calm summer evening, this had never happened before.

I said, 'I don't know the details of his death.'

'Heart attack. Let's have another drink before she comes in.' He took my glass and poured another large measure of whisky.

Judith entered the room vigorously rubbing her hair with a towel. She sat beside me on the couch.

Gerald smiled at her. 'She's just won a good role in a television film.' Gerald owned a television production company. He advised the government on cultural matters. It seemed to me that Judith would never be short of work while their relationship lasted.

'What did you want to tell me, Gerald?'

He looked at me, coldness clouding his eyes like powder in water. 'I want you back in the fold.'

'I didn't expect or want anything from your father, and you shouldn't expect anything from my mother.'

'Grow up.'

I left a pause. 'Your father was working on a book?'

'Yes. His memoirs.'

'And that girl was helping him?'

'One of his students at King's.'

'She tells me it was completed. She'd like to finish preparing the manuscript for publication.'

'Well, other people can do that.'

'I think she has a right.'

'No. Some girl wanting to make her name. It's not going to happen.'

I went to a matinee and then for a quick drink with some friends from the cast. Afterwards, I drove up Kingsway into Southampton Row. If I could persuade Gerald to hand over the papers and manuscript, it would be a sort of victory. I rang Rachel's number and told her that I needed to know more about my stepfather's book. I agreed to meet her at her parent's house in Hampstead.

The house was Georgian and handsome but a little rundown. The door was opened at length by a worried-looking middle-aged woman with long grey hair tied back in a ponytail.

'Please come in,' she said. 'Rachel should be home soon.'

She took me into the living room. 'I'm Rachel's mother. Would you like a cup of tea?'

'No, thanks.'

She spoke rapidly in an upper-class accent.

'Are you at the university?' she said.

'No.'

'Rachel gave up her flat recently. She needs to find a job. One can't remain a student forever.'

I nodded.

'I don't mean to pry. We see so few of Rachel's friends. How well do you know her?'

I hesitated.

'I'm sorry,' she said, 'it's just that Rachel had an abortion last year and she wouldn't tell us who the father was.' She laughed.

'It wasn't me. We've only known each other a short time.'

'Oh dear, I shouldn't have told you that. Please don't let on I told you.'

'Of course not.'

She was looking out of the window. 'Here's Rachel now.'

Rachel took me upstairs.

'Would you like to stay for dinner?' her mother called after us.

'No, he can't stay,' Rachel said.

She sat on her bed. She was smartly dressed in a white blouse and short black skirt. 'I've been to an interview,' she said. 'Can I stay with you until I find a place? I'll go mad if I stay here.'

'Yes, you can stay with me.' Perhaps desire is always an error of judgment.

She didn't speak until we were at my house.

'Until I find somewhere else,' she said. 'I'll take the couch.'

'Would you like something to drink?'

'If you like.'

I fetched a bottle of red wine and two glasses. The light was fading; Rachel's white blouse stood out in the half-darkness. We drank the wine quickly, glass after glass until the bottle was empty. I sat beside her on the couch. I placed my hand on her right thigh. She uncrossed her legs and opened them a little. Otherwise, she didn't move, just stared down at my hand. I started to undo the buttons of her blouse. She fell onto her back, her arms above her head, looking at me. The whites of her eyes glowed in the dusky light, the pupils were black dots. I parted the blouse. I felt if she didn't join in soon, I couldn't continue. I kissed her mouth. Her arm came down and she wriggled her skirt up above her hips. I buried my face in her hair, my eyes closed. Her body was warm and comforting. It was too late to stop.

Sussex and King's Cross

The following afternoon, we drove to a small town on the Sussex coast and spent a night and a day in a hotel on the promenade. We listened to the voices of passers-by on the front below, the hubbub of the beach, the crunch of feet on pebbles. At night to the sea murmuring.

I asked her about my stepfather.

'I was in his seminar group: he offered a few of us paid research work. He was charming, everyone liked him.'

'You had an abortion last year.'

'Who told you that? My stepmother told you that?'

'Is it true?'

'That I had an abortion and Robin was the father? Is that what you're thinking?'

'No, don't be absurd.'

We hardly spoke on the journey back to London.

At King's Cross, drunken boys, shirtless in the night heat, were standing in the middle of the road. I turned the car into a narrow, litter-strewn street of boarded-up shops. Women waited silently beneath the streetlamps.

I said, 'I think this is a mistake.'

'Fine. Let me out.' I stopped at the curb. She stood for a moment and then started to walk back towards the Euston Road. A long saloon, shiny black in the lamplight, drew alongside her, an elbow protruding from the window. One of the women moved towards Rachel. I drove close to the other car. I heard the woman shout something. Rachel ignored her and walked more quickly. A man's balding head now leant from the car. I flashed my lights; after a second's hesitation the saloon accelerated away. Rachel jumped in beside me. I pulled away as the woman's face appeared at the window.

'What the fuck are you doing?'

'He offered me three hundred quid,' she said.

She was looking at me, her thighs naked and restless on the leather seat.

'Tell me I'm a whore.'

I looked out at the familiar sights, the buildings, the kebab van, the spire of a church, the long window of mannequins. She looked at me with hooded eyes, her lipstick black at the corners of her mouth. I turned into Polygon Road.

Islington and Somers Town

'My actors don't want to be in this play,' Tom Madden said.

I followed him into a large rehearsal room.

'We can't pay you much, but you may find writing the music interesting.' He was an old friend from university; I didn't need the money, but I was happy to do him a favour.

I sat by the windows while Madden interviewed three actresses. Down in the street, cars moved bumper to bumper like the particles of a single substance. Another actress had arrived. I glanced across and saw Judith. When Madden introduced us for some reason we both pretended to be strangers. After she had left, Madden said, 'She was good. I think she'd fit.'

I went down to the street and rushed after Judith, catching up with her as she reached the corner. We went into a nearby square where she sat on the grass and took out an apple and a can of Diet Coke. 'Did you know I was working on this show?' I asked.

'No. Did you know I was?'

'You're not yet.'

She ate her apple. 'What do you think of the play?'

'I think it's prurient.'

She shrugged. 'It's a good part.'

I drove her back to Chelsea. I returned home to find Gerald sitting with Rachel in the living room.

'You never come here Gerald,' I said.

'I left messages. You didn't ring back.'

Rachel stood up and went into the bedroom.

'So, when did it happen, you and her?'

I left a pause. 'What do you want?'

'Mother's birthday...' We spoke for half an hour. I was happy to close the door on him. Rachel was standing at the window.

'What happened?' I asked

'He wasn't pleased to see me here.'

Below Gerald was wiping dust off the roof of his silver Mercedes. A plane's blinking green light drifted across the azure and pink sky. I kissed Rachel's neck. She ignored my kisses. I looked into the pink hollow of her ear. The car glided away. Her earlobes and cheeks were flushed. I felt with my lips the line of her jaw, the bone beneath the skin, the fragility of a face, and suffered a sudden macabre pang of mortality: a fear that she would die. I withdrew from her. Darkness pursued the last light around the walls of the room; Rachel stood with her back to the window, watching me, a half-smile upon her lips. The sunlight passed across her like a spotlight. She said, 'What's the matter?'

'I feel odd.'

After a slight pause, she said, 'I'm pregnant.'

I looked at her. She rocked her hips, tearful and smiling at the same time. She was like a little girl stubborn in her determination to do what she liked.

'I thought you were on the pill.'

'I never said that.'

'You never said you weren't.'

'You never asked. What do you want from me? I

give you everything, what else is there? If you don't like me, I'll leave.'

'I don't want you to leave.'

South Oxfordshire

The day before Mother's birthday I returned to the North Wessex downs. The house was deserted. I walked through the empty rooms, rediscovering the building. I went into a bedroom where there were signs of human activity – an unmade bed and scattered clothes. Then, as I approached the window, I saw the author of the mess: in the deep blue water of the pool Judith was swimming. She swam a single length beneath the surface then strolled away across the grass, using all ten fingers to comb the water from her hair.

I walked downstairs and into the garden. She was now lying in a hammock strung between two trees, one arm behind her head, the other holding a paperback above her sunglasses. With one leg she set the hammock gently swinging. 'Where's my mother?' I called.

'She's gone with Gerald to have her dog put down.'

I went back inside and poured myself a whisky, downed it, then another, then a third. When I returned to the garden Gerald and my mother were there and dinner was nearly ready. Gerald smiled and patted me on the back. I kissed Mother on the cheek. 'I'm sorry about your dog,' I said.

We sat around a table in the humid early evening. The housekeeper brought out food and wine. The red sun made a slow diagonal descent towards the horizon of trees.

'Where's Rachel?' Gerald asked.

'She's working today. She's coming down tomorrow.'

'Will you stay until Sunday?' Mother asked.

'Yes. I hope you'll be nice to Rachel.'

Gerald said, 'I think we were all under strain at the funeral.'

'I'm glad you're here,' Judith said. When she smiled her upper lip curled upwards a little.

Gerald went into the house to fetch another bottle

of wine.

'Do you mind if I smoke?' Judith asked.

'I'll have one too,' I said.

I handed her a cigarette and then lit it with a match. Judith played with her hair, lifting it away from her neck as though she intended to tie it up. Gerald came back with the wine and a gas lamp. He ignored the cigarettes; nevertheless, Judith held her cigarette vertically and blew the smoke out of the corner of her mouth.

There was an uncharacteristic calmness about Gerald. He had always, in my experience, been someone who liked to be the centre of attention. But now he sat silently for long moments, contemplating Judith. He had always changed his girlfriends like he changed his cars, only more frequently. How was Judith different? Gerald's girlfriends had always been young and pretty.

It was suddenly late. Mother went to bed. We sat in silence for a while.

'Tell us about the play?' Gerald said to Judith.

'You don't want to know. You hate the theatre, remember?'

'I happen to be on the boards of several.'

'Yes, but you hate the theatre.'

'Well, I won't deny it.'

Judith was resting her feet on the edge of her chair. Gerald started to caress one of her knees as though it was the head of a puppy. They left the table and strolled arm in arm. How beautiful it was, the orchard in the moonlight, the scent of honeysuckle, this ripeness of nature in midsummer. Gerald, grey-haired, thickset, took lithe Judith in his arms and kissed her. I took off my jeans and shirt and dived into the pool. I floated on my back, looking up at the moon and stars. I didn't hear them come back. When I pulled myself out of the pool their bedroom light was on. I put my jeans back on. Judith appeared at the bedroom window. 'The water looks like bliss,' she said.

'It is.'

'Gerald's gone to the study.'

'Come and have a swim. There's some wine left.'

'All right.'

I lay beside the pool. I heard her and turned my head, watching her legs as she approached. She pulled the dress over her head but kept on her bra and knickers. She swam beneath the surface. A pupil-like reflection of the moon on the placid water was undisturbed by her fast swimming. She glided on her back, her knickers transparent, the darkness of her pubis making her body look white. I reached for the wine bottle and took a long drink. Judith climbed from the water. 'Turn round.'

I looked at her. She saw something in my eyes and said, more firmly, 'Turn round.'

I did as I was told. 'You're very...'

'What? You can turn round now.'

She was wearing her dress again. There was a long silence. 'What's your problem with Gerald? Other than the obvious.'

'When I was about fourteen Gerald came to my school sports day. We were sitting on the grass watching some event and a teacher, a young woman, was sitting nearby. She came to the school one day a week to give violin lessons. She was teaching me, and I was in love with her. She was sitting across from us on the grass. I realised that she was exchanging looks with Gerald, that he could see up her skirt. When I

36

came back a while later, they were talking together. He started something with her but quickly dumped her. She stopped working at the school.

'What am I meant to make of that?'

'I don't know.'

'Is that all?'

We laughed. Gerald emerged from the house. 'Rachel's on the phone.'

'Tell her I'll ring her tomorrow.'

'I think you should speak to her now.'

Reluctantly I went into the house. But instead of going to the phone I stayed at the open windows, listening to their conversation.

'Have you finished working?'

'Yes. How is he?'

'Fine.'

'He drinks a lot.'

She leant back on her elbows, her legs swinging open and shut. 'Do you remember going to sports day at his school?'

'Yes, I think so.'

'A teacher behaving like this?'

'Did he tell you that?' He slipped his hand behind

her calf and stroked up and down. 'Let's go to bed.'

'He was in love with her.'

'Nonsense. He said that?'

'Yes.'

'I can hardly remember her.'

I spoke to Rachel and then went back outside. 'She's at the station. She's getting a taxi.'

'We're going to bed,' Gerald said.

Rachel arrived twenty minutes later. She stood in her jeans and T-shirt, a small rucksack against her thin back.

'You were meant to come tomorrow morning.'

'I wanted to be with you.'

'Are you hungry?' She shook her head. 'Do you want to take a dip in the pool?'

'I'm tired,' she said. 'Have they gone to bed?'

'Yep.'

'Shall we?'

'In a minute.'

She sat down but could not settle. 'I'll make some coffee,' she said. I waited twenty minutes then went upstairs. She was lying on the bed still in her jeans. I joined her on the bed. She rolled against me. I pushed her away and lay against her back.

'What's the matter?' she asked

'I don't know.'

She said, 'Please hold me until I fall asleep.'

South Oxfordshire, the next day

Judith and Rachel were playing tennis on the lawn over a makeshift net. They were getting on famously, laughing and talking as the small yellow ball whizzed between them. Gerald was sitting at a table, reading the Sunday papers. Rachel turned towards him. 'Gerald, will you let me finish my work with your father? I'm good at what I do.'

'I'm sure you are.'

'Your father chose me.'

'We'll see.'

Rachel had prepared a picnic lunch. We drove a short distance to a place that gave a fine, sweeping view of the valley. I pulled off the road at the beginning of a farm track. She laid out a blanket on the verge of long grass and unpacked her picnic hamper.

I sat on a nearby haystack. The long slope of the field was dotted with these brown sugar lumps. She turned on a transistor radio. We ate sandwiches and drank warm beer and then lay down together, kissing and embracing and drifting into sleep in the grass beneath a sky of skimming clouds.

I heard an engine. A strong-looking man of about sixty was walking towards us along the edge of the field. 'Is that your car?' he shouted. 'You'll have to move it.'

I lifted my head. Perhaps it was the beer, perhaps the tone of his voice. 'Why?'

'It's blocking the track.'

'When I'm ready.'

'This is private land. You're trespassing.'

Rachel stirred sleepily.

'Are you going to move it or not?'

'In a minute.'

The farmer walked back to the track and out of sight.

'You should move it,' Rachel said. 'The look on his face.'

She started to pack away the picnic. The farmer

came back with two young men. 'It's your own fault,' she said.

The farmer watched while his sons circled me. 'Who do you fucking think you are?' one of them said. Rachel tried to intervene, and the man pushed her away, his hands flat against her breasts.

'That's enough,' the farmer said.

I looked at him. 'That was sexual assault.'

He was suddenly conciliatory. He apologised to Rachel. She accepted the apology, but I had never known such rage.

Later that day

Mother's party was held in the garden. It was humid, and the grey-green sky threatened rain. She'd invited her local friends and neighbours. An accomplished jazz band played on a small wooden platform beneath fairy lights. Lanterns prettified the garden. Mother was holding court, passing between the country bumpkins and their concrete-haired wives like a soap star.

I looked up and saw the farmer. A young girl walked behind him. Mother introduced us. 'This is my nearest neighbour, Jack Wood.'

'We've met,' I told her.

He was taken aback, but only for a moment. 'A slight altercation earlier in the day,' he said with false jollity.

'No hard feelings,' I said. We shook hands.

'I'm afraid my son went a little too far.'

'And who's this?'

'My daughter Emily.'

'Would you like a drink?' I asked her.

'No alcohol,' the farmer said.

I led his daughter away. I handed her a glass of orange juice. 'Surely you're not so young that you don't like a drink,' I said.

'My father thinks I'm a child,' she said.

I poured a little vodka into the glass. She giggled.

'How old are you?'

'Nearly fifteen.'

She was interested in the theatre, wanted to become an actress. I introduced her to Judith. I said, 'Emily should come to London.'

After the guests had left we gathered in the living room to watch a BBC profile of Mother, a montage of television clips from the 1950s, 60s and 70s over which the narrator told the official history of her life and career – her privileged upbringing; her bravery as an agent in wartime France (no details were given); her early years as one of Labour's first female MPs; her pioneering work as a minister in the Wilson governments (a glut of footage and interviews with old colleagues). Mother, to her credit, looked embarrassed, but Gerald loved it. Rachel asked her if she still thought about the war. She replied, 'Not really. It's ancient history.'

Islington

Judith was rehearsing with an actor called Patrick. Madden kept interrupting, pacing up and down. Patrick kissed and fondled Judith. Each time they repeated the scene his hands moved nearer to her breasts. He was a Mancunian with long black hair and a neat goatee.

At the end of the day she came up to me. 'Gerald's in New York. Take me to dinner?'

I took her to a nondescript Italian restaurant on Upper Street. She ordered a pizza. We drank two bottles of Chianti.

'What are you thinking?' she asked.

'Gerald won't like that guy touching you up.'

She ignored the comment. 'He's going to let Rachel complete your stepfather's book.'

'Really?'

'Yes.'

Outside the restaurant, we parted company. A young woman wearing an unbuttoned brown leather jacket appeared from a side road. She paused and smiled. She was gamine, green-eyed. She said, 'Hello Joe, you don't recognise me, do you?'

A breeze tugged at the branches of the trees beneath the streetlamps. It fingered her fringe and the corners of her skirt. She held a champagne bottle; it looked like a skittle; its weight made her lopsided.

'You've changed your hair, but of course I recognise you. Muriel.' She was one of Gerald's old girlfriends, a dancer.

'Would you like to come to a party?' She held up the champagne.

'I'm on my way home.'

'It's not late. James and the others will be there.'

'Okay, just for ten minutes.'

She led me to a grand corner house. She was kissed and embraced by friends. She drank champagne from a bottle. The largest room, on the second floor, had been cleared of furniture. On the polished wooden boards people were dancing. A white-haired man with a terrier on his lap sat at a baby grand playing tangos and show tunes. A girl sat in the corner preparing lines of cocaine.

'How's Gerald?' Muriel asked me.

'The same.'

She held out her palm; it contained a small pink pill. 'I dare you.'

'All right.' I took the pill. I followed her into another room. Here people were sitting or lying on cushions. Open windows gave out onto a narrow balcony. Drapes billowed into the blue smoke-filled room. She found a place for us to sit. I shook hands with James, a lean middle-aged man wearing a green silk shirt. I went out onto the balcony.

'Are you all right?'

I turned to see James. 'My head's swimming.'

'Are you with Muriel?'

'We met in the street. How are things?'

'Fine.'

Muriel appeared through the drapes. 'Why won't you give me a chance?' she asked James.

'Because you're too young, not ready, not good enough. Take your pick.'

She broke away. 'I'm not his favourite,' she told me. And then, tears in her eyes, 'I'm leaving, I mean it, I'm fucking leaving.'

'So leave. Go and work in Soho. Go and lap dance.'

We left the party together. At the corner of Upper Street I hailed a black cab. 'Come home with me,' she said.

'I'll drop you off.'

At the Barbican she walked ahead of me, slowly, as if apart. She took off her shoes and ran up the steps into one of the towers. The concierge returned her smile of greeting. The apartment was so pristine it was like an expensive shirt still in its wrapper. A wall of windows gave a pilot's view of the city, a map of lights split in two by a line of snaking blackness. The dome of St Paul's filled the foreground, so near it made me step back. She was sitting on a white couch at a low glass coffee table, fixing lines of coke. I said, 'You don't live here. Whose place is it?'

'Some guy. He's in Australia at the moment.'

'He gave you a key?'

'Obviously.'

'You're living here?'

'No. I knew he had some coke.'

'Who is he?'

'No one you know. He's one of the company's patrons.'

Once we were in bed I succumbed to a state of drug-induced apathy.

Soho

Muriel rang my mobile phone.

'How did you get this number?'

'From James.'

I met her in a café. She looked drained. She chain-smoked and fidgeted with her coffee cup. 'I'm knackered and in pain,' she said. 'It never ends. Class, rehearsal, performance, class. My partner dropped me. My knee hurts. I badly need coke but my supplier's disappeared. I'm going to have to go to the source and I have no money...'

'What were you playing at last night?'

'You fell asleep. I couldn't wake you.'

'I'm prepared to help you, financially, if you'll do me a favour.'

'What kind of favour?'

I wrote her a cheque. 'I want you to see Gerald.'

She looked at the cheque. 'Why?'

'My brother's in a bad relationship. Perhaps he misses you. And I think you're still in love with him.'

'He treated me badly.'

'It's been what... two years?'

'Two years, nine months.'

'So he'll want you again, won't he?'

'Will you come with me now? It's just around the corner.'

We walked to a house in Soho Square. The bouncer in the hall responded to Muriel straight away and led us up the stairs. He went up to a short young man in a blue suit. The man spoke to the bouncer in Russian. 'I've seen her before,' he said. He pointed at me. 'Who's that?' he said in English.

'My boyfriend,' Muriel said. She was smiling. I realised she was nervous, excited or both. Her face looked swollen, childlike. We went to a room on the second floor. A red Persian rug; a leather sofa on either side. The Russian indicated that we should sit opposite him.

'I'm Peter. We can make an arrangement, but it has to be long-term.'

I laughed. 'You want us to open an account?'

'Why not? It will include a discount if she gives me something.'

I took hold of Muriel and pulled her out of the room. 'What's your problem?' she said.

'You don't have to go to these lengths.'

'I'm going back in.'

'Fine.'

'Will you wait?'

'No. I'll ring you about that favour, okay? I've given you a lot of money.'

She nodded. 'My knees are wrecked. I have to perform tonight.' She went back into the room.

Islington

'That was a disaster,' Gerald said. 'It's never going to transfer to the West End. Judy was good, though.'

We were at the first night party. 'What did you think of Patrick?' I asked.

'Patrick?'

'The male lead.'

'He's appallingly bad. Where's Rachel?'

'She's in Cambridge for a few days.'

'Working on my father's book?'

'Yes. Thank you for changing your mind about her.'

Judith was talking to the farmer's daughter.

'She's staying with us,' Gerald said. 'It was Judy's idea. Wood's daughter wants to be an actress.'

I sought out Patrick. He was drinking heavily.

'You see that young girl with Judith? She's a big fan. Saw you in that soap. I'll introduce you.'

I felt a hand on my shoulder and turned. It was Muriel. I smiled. 'Good, you came.'

'Of course. You invited me.'

'Are you high?'

'No.'

'Has he seen you yet?'

She shook her head.

'Remember, I didn't know you were coming. Patrick invited you. You didn't know about Judith and Gerald, so bumping into him here is a complete surprise.'

'Stop treating me like a child.'

'Okay. He mustn't see us talking, so… good luck.'

I left her just as I caught sight of Gerald. I took him a glass of champagne. 'You'll never guess who's here,' I told him.

I pointed at Muriel.

'What's she doing here?'

'I don't know.'

He looked at her.

'Have you seen her since?'

'No.'

'How long has it been?'

'Two years.'

'I always wondered why you dumped her. You were together for quite some time, almost a record for you.'

'What are you trying to say?'

'Nothing. Have I hit a nerve?'

He was calm again. 'No. But, really, you know nothing about me, and less about Muriel. Excuse me.'

He walked away through the crowd and went up to Muriel. A look of surprise in her eyes; a hand-shake; smiles. He took her to one side, to a couch beneath a large mirror in which I saw a distorted reflection of myself. Her knees, pressed together, were like white knuckles: she looked vulnerable.

Judith appeared in the mirror. She held an empty champagne glass. 'You were terrific,' I said.

'I don't think so. I've puked so many times my knees are like jelly.'

'I wouldn't lie to you.'

'Who's that with Gerald?'

'Your predecessor.'

She paused to take this in. 'Really?'

'Yes. Muriel. A dancer. They were together for two years. He didn't tell you?'

'He doesn't talk about his past relationships.'

Pause. 'Looks a little like you, doesn't she?'

'You flatter me.'

'No.'

'What's she doing here?'

'She must know someone. Why don't you go over and embarrass Gerald?'

'I don't think he gets embarrassed. He can talk to an old girlfriend, can't he?'

'Sure.'

At that moment Gerald kissed Muriel on the cheek and rose from the couch. He made his way across the room. He smiled and kissed Judith's neck. 'She cornered me. Sorry. On your big night too.'

'Joe has been telling me all about her.'

'He doesn't know anything about her.' He paused, his irritation hanging in the silence. 'He used to want to sleep with her, that's all. He wants to sleep with all my girlfriends.'

'I know,' Judith said.

Gerald glared at her. 'I think I better take you home.'

'Where's Emily?' Judith asked.

'Last seen with your co-star,' I said.

'Please put her in a taxi before you leave.'

'Sure.'

I drank a large measure of whisky. Muriel came over. Patrick was getting a group together to conclude the party at his flat. Over Muriel's shoulder I watched Emily leave with them. Muriel asked me to drive her home. In the car, she said, 'He wants to see me.'

'What did he say?'

'He asked me how I was. Said he'd ring me.'

'Good.' I realised she was crying. 'What's the matter?'

'Nothing.'

I allowed a long silence.

'I'm pathetic,' she said. 'I don't want to be alone tonight. Can I stay with you?'

'I don't think so.'

'I'm not looking for sex. I know you have a

problem.'

'I don't have a problem.'

'If you say so.'

I drove her home.

Somers Town and Hammersmith

The doorbell woke me. It was Judith. She looked angry.

'Were the reviews that bad?'

'Where's Emily?'

'Would you like a coffee?'

'Where is she?'

'She was with Patrick.'

'Don't tell me you let him take her home? I asked you to put her in a taxi.'

'It's all right. There was a group.'

'You thoughtless prick!' Her little fists smashed against my chest. I grabbed her wrists. She rested her head against my chest, her body wracked by little breaths of panic. 'What have you done?'

'It will be all right.'

'I promised her father we'd look after her.'

I drove her to Patrick's flat in Hammersmith. It was only six-thirty. It took several minutes for Patrick to respond to the bell. 'This better be good,' his voice finally said.

'It's Joseph. I'm here with Judith. Buzz us in.'

'Come back later.'

Judith pushed me out of the way. 'Let us in now!'

The living room was a mess of empty bottles, glasses, and cigarette butts in ashtrays. Patrick opened the blinds and said 'Jesus'. Judith, having taken in the room, was looking through the half-open bedroom door. Emily was lying nude and face down on the bed. Her hair covered her face like a pile of straw.

'What's the matter?' Patrick asked.

'She's fourteen.'

'She told me she was seventeen.'

'You're going to jail.'

Judith went into the bedroom and slammed the door.

'What's her problem?'

I sat on the couch. 'She's responsible for the girl.'

'What will she do?'

The door opened. Judith ignored Patrick and spoke to me. 'You'll have to carry her.'

Patrick said: 'What are you going to do, Judith? We have to perform tonight. You're not going to call the police, are you?'

Judith had dressed the girl. I picked her up, trying to keep my face away from her hair because it smelt of vomit. 'I think you should make a call,' I told Patrick as we left the flat.

'My agent? Talk her round, mate, yeah?'

'I'm not your mate.'

Going down in the lift, Judith said, 'We'll take her to your place.'

The girl moaned, 'Where am I? What's happening?'

'It's all right, sweetheart.'

'Is she hurt?' I asked.

'I don't know. Just drunk, I think.'

'Why my place? Shouldn't we have called the police upstairs?'

'I need to think.'

In the car she tried to reach Gerald on the phone,

but his mobile was switched off.

I waited in the living room while Judith saw to the girl. It took half an hour for her to reappear.

'Everything all right?'

She grimaced.

'You're still angry with me. I'm truly sorry.'

Judith sat on the couch. 'I don't know what to do. I can't reach Gerald.'

'You must call the police.'

'But this is going to cause such a mess. We were looking after her.'

'You mean it could be awkward for Gerald.'

'I just want to speak to him first.'

'I'll call the police. He can't blame you then.'

'Why did you let this happen?'

'I made a mistake. You can tell her old man I'm to blame, all right? We'll take her back to your house, then I'll call the police.'

'I'd rather they came here.'

'It will just confuse them. You need to be at home.'

Judith looked at me and said, 'Fine.'

Somers Town

I spent a week in Berlin to complete my work for the TV company and to pack up the few items I had left there. While I was there, I made a decision about Rachel.

'I think you should have an abortion,' I said. 'I don't want to break up with you but I'm not ready to have a child.'

She looked at me for a long time.

'I realise it was cruel, to just say it like that. I'm sorry.'

'I won't have an abortion,' she said. 'I don't want to be with you anymore.'

She went to pack her things. I let her go.

I drank all evening in one of the local pubs. I tumbled out into the street. As I approached my house, I sensed movement in the darkness to my right and turned to see two men. A fist pummelled my face. I slumped onto my knees. The last thing I saw was the boot swinging towards my head.

Royal Free Hospital, Camden

I became aware of a blurry shape. Slowly a white room materialised around me. A woman was holding my hand; she was calling for someone. I realised, with a jolt, that I was lying in a hospital bed, and that the woman was Judith. A nurse rushed in from the corridor. 'He's awake,' Judith said.

Medical staff bustled around me. I felt stiff, faint, nauseous. Judith was smiling. 'Do you know who I am?'

'Yes.' My jaw was so painful I could hardly speak.

The nurse told Judith to leave. 'I'll come back later,' she said.

The doctor was happy with all the readings from the equipment. I had been in a coma for several days. They were concerned about my head, but the other injuries – cracked ribs; bruised jaw – weren't serious. They took me for a scan, and then I slept. That evening two policemen arrived. I told them that I'd been attacked by two men, that I didn't know them, couldn't describe them, that I had no idea why anyone would attack me. 'It was a random mugging, right?'

The older detective said, 'They didn't rob you. It was a beating. In fact, you were very lucky. Someone disturbed them and they ran off.'

'Perhaps they mistook me for someone else?'

'Perhaps.' He handed me his card. 'If you think of anything that might help, give me a call.'

Judith returned as promised. 'The doctor says you're going to be okay. How do you feel?'

'Fine.'

'Why were you attacked?'

'I don't know.'

She looked at me as though I was a boy who was not telling the whole truth.

So I quickly changed the subject: 'What happened to Marcus?'

'Nothing. Gerald fixed things with Wood.'

'What do you mean?'

'Wood agreed not to take things further.'

'And you were happy with that?'

'No, not really. Wood gave the girl a beating.'

She stood and started to rearrange the flowers in the vase by the window.

'I'm sorry about the play.'

'It was for the best. I couldn't have continued with Marcus.' Finally, she left the flowers alone and looked at me until I looked back. 'Joe, where's Rachel?'

'I don't know. It's over between us.'

'I'll ring Rachel, make sure she's okay.'

'As you like.'

She raised her head. We could hear Gerald's patrician voice: he was laying down the law to some nurse or doctor. A moment later I felt his hand on my shoulder. 'What a relief,' he said. He placed a bottle of malt whisky on the bedside table.

He sat in the chair beside the bed. 'So, what's the story?'

'The police think it was a random mugging.'

'No they don't.'

'What else?'

'You tell me.'

'We should go,' Judith said. 'Joe needs to rest.'

'You go on ahead. I won't be a moment.'

Gerald watched her leave.

'Why didn't you put that girl in a taxi?'

'I've apologised to Judith.'

'I'd hate to think you were playing games.'

'Listen, she was your responsibility, not mine.'

After a moment's reflection he said, 'Okay. But you're not Wood's favourite person. You should apologise to him. He's ex-army, a respected figure in the county, and Mother's nearest neighbour.'

I had other ideas. 'Gerald, do me a favour and talk to the doctor. I want to get out of here as soon as possible.'

He nodded. 'Anything else?'

'No.'

Soho

I discharged myself from the hospital two weeks later and spent a further week alone in my house, resting and thinking. The pain in my side restricted my movements, but otherwise I felt fine.

Judith called. 'I've spoken to Rachel. She's going to travel for a while.'

'On her own?'

'With friends.'

'Good.'

The winter came. I travelled to Oxfordshire for Christmas but stayed only one night. Then, in February, I visited the Russian called Peter in Soho Square. The minder took me to a large room on the top floor of the house. Peter rose from his chair to greet me. 'What can I do for you? They tell me you have a proposition.'

'More a request.'

'This is my associate.' A stocky, black-eyed man nodded nonchalantly in my direction. The windows presented a view of the square in the rain; tiny Londoners scurrying hunch-shouldered in the squall; men in suits; girls' legs darting; umbrellas unfolding like black flowers. We sat at one end of a fine, committee-sized oak table. On the far wall there was a small Degas, a painting of dancers: it looked like an original.

'I need a gun.'

'Russians are gangsters, is that it?'

'No. I'll pay, of course.'

'Besides, I'm from Belarus. You plan to handle

this yourself?'

'Yes.'

'There are professionals who will do the job for you. I can arrange that for you.'

I paused. 'I haven't decided. For now I just need a gun. Untraceable and simple to use.'

'Okay. I want you to do something for me. The reason we're talking like friends is because you brought me that dancer. I haven't forgotten.' He poured red wine into three glasses. 'I'm arranging a party in the country. An English country weekend. I need a classy girl for the cabaret, you understand? I'm thinking of this dancer.'

'Muriel?'

'Yes, Muriel.' He lifted his glass, and we drank a silent toast.

'I'll talk to Muriel, but I can't promise anything.'

'That is all I ask. There is no obligation.'

Covent Garden

Muriel didn't return my calls. I rang James. 'She's

left us to join the Royal Ballet. They think she's good enough. We'll see.'

I found her at Covent Garden, in one of the Royal Ballet's studios. She was alone in the vast space, a tiny figure dressed in black. She stood with hands on hips, panting, staring at her reflection in the wall of mirrors.

'You've gone up in the world,' I said.

She shrugged.

I sat at the grand piano. 'What level are you?'

'Soloist. This is a real opportunity for me. If I apply myself. I'm a bit rusty.'

'Why haven't you returned my calls?'

'I've been busy. Coming here hasn't been easy. I started out here, so they know me, but they made me audition. I feel lucky they've taken me back, though. I was at the end of my tether. I know I'll have to work hard. Why are you smiling? Don't mock me. I'm a good dancer and I'm still young.'

'I know. You're beautiful. Are you making friends?'

'I've only been here a week, but yes.'

'Have you seen Gerald?'

'I don't want to talk about that.'

'Come on, there are two things that you and I talk about, Gerald and the white stuff.'

I placed a small packet on the glossy ink-black surface of the piano.

'I'm all right at the moment.'

'You're all right?'

'Yes.'

I played a few chords. I could see the tension in her body as she tried to resist the coke. She walked over to the piano. Suddenly, she picked up the packet and hid it behind her back. An elegant middle-aged woman had entered the studio. To my amusement, Muriel stood like a schoolgirl caught out by her headmistress. The woman walked over. 'Hello, Joseph.'

I shook her hand. 'Hello, Alice. It's good to see you.'

Alice turned towards Muriel. 'Is your knee troubling you?'

'No.'

'You're not just saying that?'

'No. The physio says it's fine.'

'Good. Maria's unwell, she can't dance Lescaut's Mistress tonight. What do you think?'

'That's terrible.'

'Want to do it?'

'Me?'

'You know the role.'

'Yes, kind of, but…'

'Don't worry, it will be fine.' A male dancer had entered the studio. 'Paul's here. We'll go through the *pas de deux* a few times.'

I started to leave. 'Joseph, wait. You can play for us. The music's over there.'

They spent an hour rehearsing the complex choreography. Afterwards, Alice asked to see me in her office.

'Are you with Muriel?'

'No.'

'Why are you here?'

'I'm a friend.'

'Is she still with your brother?'

'No.'

'What was in the packet? Cocaine?'

'I don't know.'

'I've known Muriel since she was a little girl. She was the most gifted dancer in her year at the school, but she's never come close to fulfilling her potential. Even as a teenager she kept getting herself into trouble. She lacks self-discipline and self-belief. I'm determined to change this. I hope her friends will help me?'

'Yes.'

I went to find Muriel. She was sitting at a table on the roof terrace.

'What did the cow want?'

'She's concerned about you. She saw the packet.'

'Fuck. She's been on my back since I was eight.'

'Don't worry. Just keep your head down.'

'How do you know her, anyway?'

'I worked here for a while as a pianist.'

'What are you doing here now, Joe?'

'I told you. Our agreement. Have you seen Gerald?'

'Yes, we met. He bought me lunch.'

'And?'

'It was before Christmas. He hasn't called.'

'So call him. Make yourself available. Ring him

now and tell him you're dancing tonight. It's a big moment. Keep at him.'

'I need to concentrate on my dancing.'

'Give back the coke I gave you.'

'No, I need it. More than ever now that I have to perform. I feel sick.'

'Precisely. Have you been back to Soho Square?'

She looked at me, her green eyes widening. 'No.'

'I saw the Russian. He has a proposition.'

'I don't understand… Do you work for him now?'

'No.'

'Does he think I'm a prostitute and you're my pimp?'

'I'm sorry. I said I'd pass on a message, that's all. He wants you to attend a weekend party he's arranging. He'll make it worth your while. Go and see him if you're interested.'

She looked away. I felt ashamed.

The South Bank

Back in the summer I had asked a journalist friend

to take a look at Gerald's business affairs and personal life. It was worth a punt. As I walked across Waterloo Bridge, my friend called me with the best news possible. Jackpot!

'Gerald's got money problems,' he said. 'His business is collapsing and he's about to be charged with fraud. What's more, we have snaps of him with a dancer from the Royal Ballet.'

'What kind of snaps?'

'Kissing her in the doorway of her place. It's not a huge story but it's fun given that he has friends in high places.'

'Have you spoken to Gerald?'

'Not yet. But it's only fair we give him a chance to lie about it. This was what you wanted, right? I thought you'd be pleased.'

'I am pleased. When will it run?'

'Tomorrow or the next day. We're going to combine both stories. He's finished.'

Judith was waiting beneath the trees, almost unrecognisable in her woollen hat and overcoat. We went to the end of one of the narrow wooden jetties that stretched out into the Thames.

'You look well,' she said.

'I am. How's Gerald?'

'Fine.'

I wondered if she knew. I wanted to warn her, but I didn't want to warn him.

'I've received an email from Rachel,' she said. 'She wants me to tell you... Perhaps I shouldn't tell you...'

'What?'

'She's had an abortion. She's met someone. She wants you to know that she won't be coming after you with a baby.'

I tried not to show my distress, but she could tell. She touched my arm tenderly. 'I'm so sorry.'

'Fuck it, it's for the best. I'll get those drinks.'

I went into the bar and drank two shots of whisky before returning with our beers.

'If you love Rachel, you should tell her,' she said.

'The truth is, I've never loved anyone. Now and again, I want someone. I want you. You've been teasing me for months.'

'That's not fair. Don't treat me like this, I don't deserve it.' She rose. 'You're being mean to me because you're upset about Rachel. I hope you accept this before it's too late.'

South Oxfordshire

I left my car down a secluded track not far from my mother's estate. It had been snowing all day and the white landscape was eerily visible against the black sky. I followed a footpath beside a ploughed field. The path took me through a copse of old elms. As the trees thinned, I reached for a pair of binoculars. Below, in a hollow of the down, there was a farm. I looked at its centrepiece, a handsome three-storey house. In an upstairs room I could see a girl, combing her hair: Emily. The front door opened and the brothers appeared and stepped into a Range Rover. I walked across the fields, steadily climbing until I reached a point that gave a view of the road that led to the village. The road crossed a railway cutting. On one side there was a petrol station; on the other, a driveway led to a large roadside pub that rose above the chasm like a sinister house in a horror film. I watched through the binoculars as the Land Rover pulled off the road and into the pub car park, its tail-lights blinking; and as the brothers swung from its cabin and marched into the building. A train hummed and rattled in the cutting. After it had passed the silence was absolute.

The white downland, across which, in the far distance, the illuminated toy-sized train silently sped, was like an undiscovered country. I walked back to my car and wrapped myself in a duvet. I'd brought two flasks of coffee and sandwiches. I ate, listened to the radio, and slept. Soon enough it was time. I walked back to the vantage point. Customers were leaving the pub. I ran down the hill, my boots scuffing up snow and hard mud. I skirted around the farm and walked through the trees that lined the long private lane. I held the heavy black pistol in my hand and waited.

I heard the Range Rover and then saw its lights. I walked calmly out into the lane and the car jolted to a halt. For a few seconds I stared at the brothers, and they stared back. I wanted them to recognise me. Snow fell. I knew that further hesitation would be fatal. I raised the gun and fired two shots through the windscreen. Blood splattered against the glass. I opened the door and fired a second bullet into each shaven head. Then I walked slowly back through the trees to my car.

London

By the summer I was spending most weekends in Oxfordshire. My mother had exiled Gerald. He had disgraced the family; a grave error from someone who wasn't a blood relative. During the week, in London, I concentrated on my work.

Judith had left Gerald. She was dating a famous actor. She wouldn't see me. One night in early June I intercepted Muriel at the Opera House stage door and asked her to come for a drink.

'No.'

We stood in a Floral Street doorway as the crowds streamed by.

'Something to eat, then.'

She shook her head. 'So, you got what you

wanted,' she said.

'I'm sorry you were drawn into it.'

'No, you're not.'

'Did the press hound you?'

'I'm not important enough. Anyway, I don't care about these things. I just want to dance now.'

'Can we see each other?'

She looked at me for a long time. 'I don't think so. We're going on tour to Japan, so I won't be around until the autumn anyway.'

'I've come through a crisis. I've changed.'

'I don't want you to change.' She smiled and walked away.

I waited for the police to track me down. They never did. The brothers had been dealing drugs and the investigators decided that they were the victims of a rival gang. Wood put the farm up for sale and moved what remained of his family to Australia. I persuaded my mother to buy it. The estate now stretched from the downs to the river.

I emailed Judith asking her to tell Rachel that I wanted to see her. Several more messages were sent and received, and it was September before Judith emailed to say that Rachel had agreed. The meeting place was the garden at the centre of a north London square. When I arrived, the garden was deserted. The branches of the tall chestnuts shook and jerked in the wind. The wooden benches looked like forlorn pieces of sculpture symbolising absence and loss. Around the garden the Georgian terraces looked equally vacant. I wondered whether she was watching me. I sat on the arm of a bench and lit a cigarette. The hours passed and the light started to fade. I waited.

The gate creaked. I turned and thought I saw, in the gloom at the far side of the garden, someone at the gate; but almost at once the ghostly shape vanished. The gate continued to creak. I waited. I looked up at the houses. Beneath the sloping roofs and tall chimney stacks lights were being switched on in some of the rooms. Rachel appeared at a window cradling a child in her arms.

Four Stories

The Portrait

She was younger than the others and a stranger to them. She paced nervously on the white path between the lime trees. One of the senior women walked up to her and seized hold of her hair. 'Who are you?' Her rouged mouth smelt of wine. 'You can't stay here.' The woman scrutinised the girl's plain dress, peasant boots and bare legs. As the girl resisted, her boots scuffed up dust that dirtied the pale blue high-heeled shoes of her attacker. The woman wrestled her to the ground. 'Go home to your family before it's too late. If you're still here when I come back, I'll have you tied in a sack and thrown in the river.'

The girl straightened her dress and retied her hair. In the green gloom beneath the trees she became aware of another figure. 'What are you looking at?' she cried. 'Leave me alone.'

The boy stepped closer. 'She roughed you up. I'm sorry. I'm Luc, you know me.'

'Can you pay?' She held out the flat of her palm.

He followed the girl beside the river. A swinging lantern on a barge broke the darkness. The wind was filled with snow. 'Please, Monsieur, leave me alone.'

'Come home with me.'

'You'll take me home? You're mad.'

'I have food, wine. It's cold out. I'll find you some money, I promise.'

'I can't. I must do as I'm told.'

'I'm an artist. I'll draw you. There are bookshops that will buy drawings of a girl like you.'

'You'll cheat me. You'll keep the picture for yourself.'

'No. I'll draw many pictures of you. I can draw quickly. I'll show you where to sell them.'

'Where do you live?' He pointed at the huge black edifice of the Louvre palace. 'They won't let me in there!'

'I'll let you in. You'll be with me.'

She said she was tired, so he carried her on his back. 'Tell me your real name,' he said. She shook her head. 'Then I won't take you.'

'Madeleine.'

Suddenly, further down the quay, they saw the flame of a lantern. It was too late to avoid the two figures who appeared in its light. The leader was as compact and as straining to be aggressive as a fighting dog. His companion was tall and bony beneath his wide-brimmed hat. His hand rested in the pocket of his long coat. Madeleine slid off Luc's back but stayed close to him. She tugged Luc's jacket and whispered, 'Don't provoke them.' The leader held the lantern close to the girl's face.

'I have to go with them,' she said. But Luc wouldn't back down. The brief beating that followed left him curled in the mud.

Luc followed the lantern. The two men took Madeleine into a building with barred windows. Opposite, where a barge was moored, an elderly man was sitting with his dog beside a brazier. The man called to his wife to bring water to clean the boy's wounds. 'I'm Bazin, boatman,' the old man said.

Madame Bazin inspected Luc's ribs and washed the blood from his face. 'What happened to you?'

'The police. They took my girl.' He pointed at the building.

The old man nodded. His wife crossed the street and banged on the door until it was opened.

'What can your wife do?'

'We know them.'

Ten minutes later Madame Bazin returned with Madeleine. Madeleine wouldn't let Luc touch her in front of the old couple. 'What did they do to you?' he demanded.

'Nothing.'

Madame Bazin took Madeleine onto the barge and below deck. When they re-emerged, she told Luc, 'She's only fourteen.' Luc shrugged.

'Will you still take me home?' Madeleine asked.

They crossed the river and the place du Louvre. As they entered a stairwell one of the caretakers blocked their way. 'You can't bring her in here,' the man said. 'Lapierre will hear of it. He'll relieve you of your position.'

Luc shoved the man to one side and led

Madeleine up the stairs, calling down, 'You know Lapierre now sits on the police committee? I'll denounce you as a royalist. Then he'll relieve you of your head. What do you think of that?' By the time Luc had reached the top of the building, and saw that the man was still standing, as if paralysed, at the foot of the stairs, he felt ashamed. He left Madeleine in his small attic room. 'You can stay here as long as you want,' he said. 'I have to work but I'll return as soon as I can.'

In the studio, Luc's fellow apprentice Jean was mixing paints and preparing the day's work. Jean looked up and shook his head as Luc slumped down on a chaise longue under the skylights. Jean emulated Lapierre by keeping his sleeves clean, his waistcoat buttoned, and his cravat tied. Luc wore paint-splattered clothes, and his fingers were perpetually stained.

They could hear the unmistakable approach of their master. 'She's late again,' Lapierre shouted. He pointed at Luc. 'You, boy, button your waistcoat and go and see where she is.' Luc went to an alcove with a view of the place du Louvre. Far below, the tiny figures of Isabelle Desgraves and her maid were running from a carriage across the vast grey surface of the square. 'She's here. She's climbing the stairs.'

The two young women entered the studio in such a hurry that they slid laughing across the polished parquet floor. Then they saw Lapierre. 'Monsieur, forgive me,' Isabelle said. 'The traffic, the traffic, I swear… You know how chock-a-block Paris gets at this hour.'

'It is half past eight. You were expected at eight-fifteen. Take up your position.'

Isabelle sat down on the chaise longue.

'You look flushed, Madame. Where have you been?'

'Running, because I was late.' She was close to tears.

'Are you crying?'

'Have I offended you?'

'You arrive late for the fourth time in a row.'

'I was only ten minutes late.' Fighting back, she said, 'You're being paid for your time, Monsieur. And your fee is very high. You make me look like a child. And plain! I look plain in your painting. And you make me appear before this plain background. There is no life.'

'Shall I return the money to your husband and burn the painting?'

'Forgive me. Sometimes I don't think before I open my mouth.'

'This must end anyway. This will be our last session.'

'Are you really prepared to give up on me? I think you must be angry indeed. The sitting has gone on for so long. It has been so tiring. I've had to get my courage up just to come here.'

'I'm becoming more active in public life. I have to be circumspect in accepting commissions. I cannot be seen to be painting the wrong kind of people.'

'Oh, I see. Am I in that category?'

'Your husband is a financier. Reputable people have denounced him.'

'It is said you're taking revenge on the people you painted.'

'I sign warrants as a member of the Committee. I shouldn't tell you this, but your husband will be arrested later today. You shouldn't go home. If you're there they could arrest you too.'

'I won't abandon my husband.'

'He's an old man. You're better off without him. Please do as I say.'

She shook her head and reached for Alice's hand. 'I must warn him,' she said. She paused at the door and looked at Lapierre. 'Why have you made me come here these last weeks? To toy with me? You're a monster.' She didn't wait for a reply.

Isabelle arrived home to discover men ransacking through her husband's books and papers. He had been taken away. She was arrested and transported to a prison near Saint-Geneviève. She prepared herself for ridicule, violence and even rape, but the officials and guards were respectful. She was allowed to sit on a chair in the vestibule while the paperwork was completed. The communal rooms and small cells to which she was taken were crowded with women of all ages, who slept on pallets or makeshift beds of straw. One of the women told her that if she wanted to go to her death looking her best, she should change into a prison dress and only back into her fine clothes when her name was called, and if she wanted to avoid the indignity of having her hair shorn by a man, she should let one of them cut her hair to reveal her neck. Isabelle agreed.

'What happens now?'

'It's best you don't think about that,' the woman replied.

'Please, I'd rather prepare myself.'

'There's a roll call every morning. These last days they've been taking dozens of people at a time.'

With her hair cut short and her body encased in a simple grey smock, Isabelle felt like a different person, which, she knew, was just as well. Most of her fellow prisoners were also used to servants and luxury, to clean linen and expensive perfume, to fine food and soft beds. They kept themselves sane by gossiping, praying, and writing letters. Others, though, stared into space for hours. The doors were not locked and during the day the women could walk in the courtyard. At nightfall, Isabelle was handed a piece of bread and a glass of red wine. After she had eaten, she lay down on the straw-strewn floor. In the darkness it was no longer possible to be brave.

During Isabelle's third week in the prison a guard escorted her to the first floor and left her alone in a room overlooking the courtyard. A short time later Lapierre entered. He wore a blue coat and a red and white striped waistcoat, but looked dishevelled and exhausted, as if he had spent days travelling. He placed a portfolio on the table. 'I'm happy to see that, in the circumstances, you look well.'

'Why are you here?' Isabelle asked.

'I wanted to see you, to express my condolences.'

Isabelle's husband had been executed the morning following their arrest. Awaiting her own death, she was stoical about his. 'I don't understand you. Why do you care?'

Lapierre paced the room, while Isabelle sat patiently on a chair. 'Things are not looking good for me. Today was a terrible day in the Convention.'

'You want my sympathy, Monsieur?'

'No. I want to give you hope. If my faction falls, then all this could be over for you. You'll be released.'

She slid from the chair onto her knees.

'I've been keeping you off the morning lists.' He

lifted her back onto the chair. 'I have to go.'

'Can't you escape?'

'No, I fear not.' He indicated the portfolio. 'It's for you. It contains the preliminary drawings from our first sessions, along with some other subjects that you may find of interest.'

Before Isabelle could thank him, he had departed. She untied the cover of the portfolio. Lapierre had drawn the nape of her neck, her ear, the folds of her dress. There were sketches of her profile and of her open face staring out from the page: these rushed portraits were so truthful of the young girl she had been at the moment of their creation that they startled and moved her.

The following morning, the prisoners were told that they were free to go. The women changed back into their own clothes. It was very early and there were no carriages. Rather than wait with the other women, Isabelle decided to walk home. The street descended towards the river. She had never seen the city (other than her private part of it) at this hour, the roads deserted, and the buildings shuttered and silent. The dark alleys and gaping doorways threatened danger but having escaped the executioner she felt blessed and untouchable. Slowly the darkness softened into blue, sunlight glinted off the higher windows and the streets started to fill with the first waves of working people. They stared at her as though she belonged to a different species, and, despite the degradation of the last few weeks, she instinctively felt the same. She crossed the river by the Pont-Neuf and was soon in the narrow, permanently shaded streets of her home quarter.

The gateman smiled with relief when he saw her, and the housekeeper wept and followed her from room to room. 'It's going to be all right, Marie. Where's Alice?'

'She went to her father's.'

'Send the boy to fetch her. Bring me hot water. I need to wash before breakfast.'

'Yes, Madame. It is a joyous day.'

Alone in the grand second-floor drawing room, Isabelle looked at a portrait of her husband and then at her reflection in the glass. For the first time in her life, she felt free.

They came for Luc while he and Madeleine were

enjoying the early spring sunshine, lying together in a grove of chestnut trees, listening to the bells of Saint-Sulpice. 'Do you like it here, Mademoiselle?'

'Yes, Monsieur.'

'We could be in the country.'

'What do you know about the country?'

He was looking at the tricolour ribbon she was wearing around her ankle. 'What's that?'

'Nothing. He makes me wear it.'

'Is he here? Take it off.'

'No. It's pretty.'

'It's time you left him.'

'You know I can't. He'll cut my throat.'

'I'll kill him.'

'You're just a boy.'

And then, quietly, from opposite sides of the grove, the men appeared. 'It will be alright,' he told her as he was taken away. She looked for him for many days. She went to all the prisons. Finally, she asked Jean for help. Their search ended at the Châtelet morgue. An official took them into a room with a high, curved ceiling. The sickening smell of putrefaction reached them before they saw the body. The windows were small and ceiling-high but emitted enough light to reveal the chamber's flaking green walls and the body on the table. A young man, fully clothed; his head caved in, more skull than face. Jean recognised the buttons on Luc's coat. The blue material was obscured by grime and dried blood.

The official was a nondescript middle-aged man, neatly dressed in black. 'Is that him?'

Jean said, 'Yes.'

Madeleine had walked to the table. She had taken hold of Luc's hand and was staring at his face.

'What happened to him?' Jean asked.

'He was pulled from the river. Probably jumped off one of the bridges.'

'Jumped?'

'We get several drownings a week this time of year.'

'You think he committed suicide?'

'It's hard to say.'

'Look at his face.'

'Not unusual for someone who has fallen from a bridge.'

Madeleine was shaking. Jean took hold of her

shoulders and placed her away from the body.

'What do the police say?'

'What can they say? I will write in the record that the injuries suggest the possibility of murder. But also that there were no witnesses, no evidence and therefore no murderer to arrest. I need to record the death, so that the body can be handed over to the next of kin as soon as possible. I'll need his age, place of residence, occupation and place and date of birth.'

Jean nodded. Behind them Madeleine was wailing uncontrollably. She slid down the wall onto the floor.

'Who is that?'

'His friend.'

'I see. Let's complete the paperwork upstairs.'

Madeleine ran along the quays; she ran as though she was back in the sloping fields after haymaking at dusk, her brother and his friends snapping at her heels. She breathed in the evening air, and it tasted sweet after the stench of the morgue. She cared nothing for the curiosity and anger her flight was provoking. She feared only Luc's murderer. As she approached the barge, she saw that Bazin and his boy were raising the rust-coloured sail. The hound was running back and forth along the deck so excitedly that it almost toppled over the side. Madeleine leapt onto the deck and into Madame Bazin's arms.

'What is it? What's happened?'

'He killed him. He's dead. He's dead.'

The barge moved slowly away from the bank. Bazin navigated the long hull into the fast-flowing current at the heart of the river, and then allowed the boy to take over. He lit his first pipe of the voyage and watched his wife as she rocked the weeping girl in her arms. They headed south.

The Encore

That winter, the last of the war, the river froze over,
and stray dogs died where they lay. The scarcity of
wood meant that fires could only be lit for a few
hours a day. Even in the wealthy quarters people had
started to break up and burn their furniture.

In an apartment in the 16th arrondissement a
young musician called Iris Dalbert wore her overcoat
and fingerless gloves as she sat at the grand piano.
She couldn't bring herself to practice; instead, she
walked over to the balcony windows and looked out
at the plane trees and the white rooftops. In the café
opposite she could see a woman sitting between two
soldiers. When the woman turned she recognised
the smiling face of a girl she had known at school.

The housekeeper came in to clear away the

breakfast Iris hadn't eaten.

'Is my father still here?'

'He left earlier than usual.'

She returned to the window. The girl was leaving the café. Her mouth seemed very red in contrast to the monochrome setting. As she crossed the street she bumped into an elderly man, sending his hat flying in a gust of wind. Iris smiled, for the old man was her teacher.

She sat on a settee and waited. When the professor entered the room he was still cursing the young woman.

'You had a lucky escape,' Iris said, taking his hat.

'Did you see?'

But he wasn't one for small talk. He pointed at the keyboard.

'Let me hear.'

'No, we've gone through these pieces a hundred times.'

'We still have to decide on the piece for the encore.'

'I have something in mind.'

'What?'

'I don't want to say.'

He was struggling to come to terms with the fact that she was no longer a child. 'This is no good. The encore is as important as the rest. But as the rest is very serious, sombre even, you should play something witty and light that will delight your audience. A Mozart or Haydn allegretto.'

Iris respected her teacher and tolerated – at least in his presence – his lack of understanding of both her and the world around them. She didn't care to pander to the collaborators who would occupy most of the seats.

To get rid of the professor she agreed to play the Mozart. Soon after his departure she walked the short distance to the Conservatoire. She waited in a long music-filled corridor for her friends Carole and Paul to emerge from class. They went to their favourite café, a small hidden-away place, and huddled together beside one of the heaters. She told them that she hadn't changed her mind and that they should meet her outside the stage door immediately at the end of the performance. Carole said, 'I don't know.'

'It will be all right. It's a small gesture.'

'They probably won't even realise,' Paul said.

They shared a packet of cigarettes. Iris hurried home in the fading light. Now that the concert was imminent she started to prepare. She sat at the piano and played a few pages of the Brahms. In her bedroom she changed into a black dress. Her father had given her a pair of stockings, but she knew where he'd got them and refused to wear them. She slipped her bare feet into a pair of expensive high-heeled shoes that had belonged to her mother.

The car came for her at five. In the theatre, after the necessary formalities, she walked onto the stage and faced the auditorium. Empty and red, it made her think of an open mouth. She turned to the piano. She was pleased. The instrument had been expertly tuned so that the tone was both warm and ringing. She retreated to the dressing room and lay down on the narrow bed to rest. She was woken by the stage manager, a young woman called Teresa. 'It's nearly time.'

'I fell asleep?'

'Yes. The professor came but didn't want to

disturb you.'

'And my father?'

'He called. He said he's been delayed.'

'It's just as well.'

'Just as well?'

She went to the mirror. 'Do I look okay?'

Teresa carefully re-tied Iris's hair and knelt to check the hem of her dress. 'You look beautiful.'

Iris followed Teresa along the corridor and down a flight of stairs into the wings. She looked at the black piano, and allowed the stacked rows of figures beyond to remain faceless, only registering that each uniform, black or grey, was separated from the next by coloured cloth, skin and diamonds. As she walked out onto the stage she looked at the piano as if it represented safety, and her acknowledgement of the audience was so brief as to be cursory. Impatient, because anxious, she began to play before the audience had settled and at once her concentration on the music was so complete that all other thoughts were pushed from her mind. At the end of her programme the applause was enthusiastic. She walked off the stage. Her teacher was pleased: he kissed her on each cheek. She walked back to the piano and began her encore, the first of Mendelssohn's *Lieder ohne Worte*. About halfway through she became aware of a murmur of anxiety. At the edge of her vision, she could see a blur of heads turning. She kept playing. A man in a black uniform had risen. He spoke in the manner of someone who was used to being obeyed, and the malignity of his stare was felt acutely by the slight girl who was its target. His words cut through the general chorus of discomfort and disapproval. 'Disgrace… How dare you play this filth? Someone stop this Jew-loving bitch…' She continued to the end of the piece, and then walked off. The old man, devastated and close to tears, slapped her. She pushed her way through the small gathering of theatre staff and ran down the stairs to the stage door.

Outside, Carole and Iris embraced, and Paul gave Iris his coat. Without speaking, they headed in the direction of the river. This close to curfew the side roads were near-deserted, and dark. A youth on a bike, speeding without lamps, swerved to avoid them. The red tip of a cigarette flared in a doorway and revealed, for a moment, a gaunt face. Their sense of elation was fragile, and such encounters spooked them. On the other side of the river, they entered a quarter of closed bookshops and small galleries. They stepped through a wooden doorway into a courtyard and climbed the stairs to an apartment on the fifth floor. The apartment belonged to the family of Paul's girlfriend, Iris's closest friend, arrested and deported to the east only a month before. The friends drank wine but spoke few words before going to bed. Early the next morning, Iris left the others sleeping and made her way home. She felt sick but mostly numb, and it was this sense of disconnection, enhanced by the silver half-light and unnatural silence, that propelled her so calmly towards the cars waiting outside her building.

The Confession of Mrs Bettencourt

Since the death of her husband, many years ago, Mrs Bettencourt had lived on her own in the manor house. The only people who entered her home were sent by the care agency, and, of these, only young Céline met her approval. This was why, when Mrs Bettencourt decided it was time to end her life, on the late summer day that marked the beginning of her ninetieth year, she chose to confess her crime to a Belgian girl she hardly knew.

Céline arrived, as usual, on her bicycle. She pedalled at speed down the avenue of old horse chestnut trees and across a gravelled forecourt that was mostly dust and weeds. The old lady was waiting at the top of the steps. 'Something different today,' she said, shambling off down the dark hall to her study at the back of the house.

On the large circular table in the centre of the room there was an old black and white photograph, a tiny metal box, a bottle of red wine, two glasses and an army revolver.

'What's going on Mrs Bettencourt?'

'I want you to do something for me. You must promise.'

'I promise.' Céline was looking at the gun. 'Is it loaded?'

'Of course it's loaded.'

'Where did you get it?'

'It's my old service revolver. I should have given it back when I was demobbed, but I was naughty.'

'During the war? You were in the army?'

'Women didn't fight in the army. I was in the Special Operations Executive. Will you take a drink with me?'

'Yes, thank you.'

'Sit down.'

Céline took off her jacket and reached for one of the wooden chairs. Mrs Bettencourt poured the wine. Céline pointed at the little box. 'Is that a snuff box?'

'No. It's a pillbox. I was twenty-one and riding in the back of a motorcar down a sunken lane with my controller. I felt like a schoolgirl again, being taken to boarding school by my father. As we arrived at the airfield, he handed me this box. It contains a cyanide pill.'

'Just like that?'

'Yes. He handed me the box as if he was giving me some pocket money. It was all so classically stiff upper lip. Do you know what that means?'

'Of course.' She emptied her glass. 'You didn't give me much.'

'I need you to stay alert.'

Céline smiled. 'You're a tough old lady, Mrs Bettencourt.'

'Well, *ma petite*, isn't that true?'

She walked over to the French windows, opened them, and then came back, a tiny, hooked figure encased in a grey gabardine overcoat.

'I'll have one of your Gitanes.'

Céline took out the packet, handed her a cigarette and lit it with a lighter. For a few moments, they smoked in silence. Finally, Mrs Bettencourt said, 'I've written a short statement. I'll sign it and you'll witness it. I want you to take it to the papers.'

'The papers?'

'*The Times* or *The Telegraph*. They'll be interested. You see, many years ago, I used to be a public figure, a politician.'

'I know. The lady in the office told me.'

'So will you do as I ask?'

'Yes.'

The soft natural light was diminishing. Mrs Bettencourt went to switch on the lights. Céline was contemplating the photograph. 'You once told me that you were interested in photography, so what do you think?' Mrs Bettencourt asked.

'An amateur shot from the 1950s, perhaps the 40s.'

'1943. France.'

'A group of young people, four men and two women. They are in a bar, I think. The man and woman in the centre look like a couple. She is reclining into his arms and gazing up at him. The other woman is younger, just a girl. She could be a waitress. It is a striking image, despite the poor quality. Cigarette smoke softens the light. The photographer has captured a moment of happiness. Who was he?'

'Oh, I can't remember. He doesn't matter. Why ask about him? It's the people in the photograph who matter. The man in the centre was called Nicholas Baume. He was the leader of a resistance group. The other men were his comrades.'

'And the women?'

Mrs Bettencourt pointed at the pillbox. 'If you look carefully at the woman you can see a little bulge near the top of her skirt.'

'She's you?'

'Yes. I kept the pillbox in the hem of my pants.'

'You were beautiful, Mrs Bettencourt.'

'Not really. It's the girl with the sad eyes that you can't stop staring at.'

'Who was she?'

'She looked like you, don't you think?'

'A little.'

'You tie your hair up in the same way. Our nationality betrays us.'

'I'm from Belgium, Mrs Bettencourt.'

Mrs Bettencourt elongated her body to reach across the table. Her right hand emerged from the oversized sleeve of her coat like a bony crab. 'I killed her with this gun,' she said.

'All right… If you say so, Mrs Bettencourt.'

Mrs Bettencourt pocketed the revolver. 'You will no longer think of me as a typical old woman. I've written it all down here.' She slid the piece of paper across the table. 'Read it. Then I'll sign it and you'll witness my signature.'

Mrs Bettencourt's statement, written in a small, neat hand on ruled paper, was short and to the point. Céline stretched her bare arm across the table and momentarily touched the old lady's hand. 'I don't know what to say.'

'Will you sign it?'

'Yes, but…Will you tell me more?'

'What do you want to know?'

The ceiling light was attached to a long flex. Mrs Bettencourt sucked on her cigarette, releasing smoke into the circle of light. Céline touched the photograph. 'Tell me about Nicholas.'

'You're thinking that we were intimate. You're right, but please don't ask me to talk about that. He was also sleeping with the girl. A number of the men were.'

'What happened to him?'

'He was arrested and shot during the last weeks of the war. All the members of the cell were executed.'

'And the girl?'

'Adine. She worked as a maid in an auberge. Not a local girl. She'd travelled south with her mother during the exodus at the start of the war. She wasn't a member of the group. One day someone saw her hurrying into the headquarters of the Milice. We snatched her on her way back and took her to the farm we used as a meeting place. We needed to interrogate her and act quickly. Do you understand?'

'Yes. I understand.'

'The girl was bullied and slapped and soon confessed that she was working for the Milice, but she swore she hadn't betrayed us. There was a slight chance that she hadn't given our names. But we couldn't let her go, knowing that she could destroy us. None of the men would do it. The girl was wailing in the barn while they argued outside. This went on into the night. Finally, I walked alone into the barn and shot the girl in the back of the head. Now do you believe me?'

'Yes.'

'I only wanted to confess to the facts, but you've forced me to relive my crime.'

'I'm sorry.'

'When I left the barn my face and blouse were splattered with blood. I won't try to justify what I did. From the moment I pulled the trigger I've thought of myself as a malignant person. The others could hardly look at me. Of course, they accused me of killing her because she was a rival and I was jealous of her.'

She lifted the bottle of wine. Her arm was quivering. Céline took the bottle from her and refilled her glass.

'That night the plane came for me and I returned to England. It was too late for the others. The girl had already talked. The Gestapo rounded them up the next day.'

Mrs Bettencourt was silent for a long while.

Céline took out her phone and checked her messages. She realised that Mrs Bettencourt was staring at her and frowning so she put the phone down on the table. Mrs Bettencourt said, 'What time is it?'

'It's half-nine.'

'Where are the others?'

'The others? We're alone, Mrs Bettencourt.'

'I think you know you've been a bad girl.'

'A bad girl? I think we should put all this stuff away.'

'I have something else to show you. In the shed at the end of the garden.'

'I should get you ready for bed. I need to leave soon.'

'Nonsense. If you're meeting one of your men, he'll have to wait.'

'One of my men? You're really on form tonight.'

'Fetch that torch, girl. Over there on the sideboard. Not that it's dark yet.'

Mrs Bettencourt stepped into the garden. Despite her frail legs, she moved steadily behind the cone-shaped beam of the torch. Céline followed her across the lawn. They went down a step and through knee-high grass. Céline said, 'Mrs Bettencourt, I'm worried that you will fall.'

'I've never fallen in my life,' Mrs Bettencourt said.

The shed was at the far end of the garden, hidden behind shrubs and trees.

'I can't see the latch, will you open it? There's a light switch on the left.'

Céline opened the door and reached for the light. She walked inside. Other than a lawn mower at the far end, and some shelves holding garden tools and flowerpots, the shed was empty. Céline looked down to see Mrs Bettencourt's elongated shadow distend beside her own across the concrete floor, the image of a gun pointing at a head, but she didn't have time to react. The sound of the shot was shattering, but Mrs Bettencourt had prepared herself for the force of the recoil and the momentary deafness.

She watched the girl's body plummet to the ground. She knew that the bullet had killed her instantly. She returned to the house. She opened a cupboard and retrieved an old brown suitcase, struggling to lift it onto the table. She raised the lid and sat before the machine, uncoiling the old cable of the headphones until she was able to place the unit over her head. After she had tapped a message in Morse code, she put the pillbox inside the hem of her underpants and left the house by the front door. 'It will be a Lysander,' she said quietly. She sat on the steps and listened out for the familiar murmur of the plane's engine.

The Last Public Hanging

Mr Carver arrived on the midday train. Inspector Raine thought that he looked unwell, more bone than flesh. Carver wanted to see the prisoner and the scaffold straight away. 'My wife and I would be honoured if you'd stay with us tonight,' Raine said. In fact, his wife was unhappy to have the hangman in her home. The Chief Constable had left Raine with no choice.

'Perhaps you would tell me something about the prisoner,' Carver said.

'Molina, an itinerant Spaniard with no English who was working as an odd-job man in a pub. He murdered the young wife of a labourer. Murdered her in her cottage.'

'The case against Molina?'

'He was seen in the village, and, when we caught him, he was wearing a coat that had been stolen from the cottage.' Raine paused. 'An appeal has been placed before the Home Secretary. There are people here who think he's innocent. I too have doubts. No witness saw him entering or leaving the cottage. There was no blood on his clothing. And he seems to be a gentle man. But perhaps I've said too much. If I was about to hang a man, I'd want to be certain of his guilt.'

'I am just a public servant, Inspector. The responsibility lies with those who try and sentence these men.'

'I arrested him,' Raine said. 'I compiled the evidence. If anyone should feel uneasy it is me.'

The redbrick walls of the prison rose from wasteland between the canal and the railway tracks. The scaffold had been constructed in front of the main gates, near the vegetable garden. Raine watched as Carver inspected the platform and checked the trap mechanism. He opened his bag and took out a length of thick rope.

'I remember the last public hanging here,' Raine

said. 'It was about fifteen years ago. I was sixteen. A young girl. Were you the hangman?'

'I was. There was a mob that day.'

Raine remembered vividly the girl's face before the brown hood was placed over her head, and he remembered the way it had been sucked into her mouth as she took her last breaths. 'That people could find something so miserable a spectacle.'

'Human nature,' Carver said.

'She took a long time to die,' Raine said. The girl had killed her baby by smearing arsenic on her nipples.

Carver remembered the girl too. Of all the ones he had dispatched in a career spanning forty years, only the first haunted him as she did. Raine led Carver into the prison. They followed a warder down one of the long corridors. 'After you've seen the prisoner, the governor requests your company for tea, Mr Carver,' the warder said. He stopped outside a cell door and slid open the spyhole. Molina was lying on the bunk, his face to the wall. His slumped body, although motionless, expressed dejection and pain. 'It's not for me to say, Mr Carver, but I find it hard to believe that a young man as quiet as he could have murdered the unfortunate woman. She was cut to pieces, Mr Carver, mutilated. Inspector Raine will tell you, he saw her.' Carver was looking at his victim. 'Will it at least be quick?' the warder continued.

Carver turned and looked at the warder coldly. 'There's no humane way of killing a man,' he said.

Raine left Carver with the prison governor and went home. Clare was playing with their son Thomas in the garden. Raine went to his study and re-read all his notes relating to the Molina case, checking for inconsistencies and peculiarities. He wanted to reassure himself of Molina's guilt. He paid particular attention to the village constable's report. The constable had been the first policeman to see the body. He had reached the scene at one-thirty. There was a detail in his report about potatoes cooking on the stove. The woman's husband, Hunt, had found her shortly before one o'clock, when he had arrived home for lunch. The doctor's report said that she had been killed between eleven and one. Molina had been seen leaving the village at twelve.

Content, Raine took his wife and son up onto the downs to fly the kite he had given the boy for his birthday. The wind swept through the grass and wrapped Clare's dark green dress against her legs. Thomas's cap was blown from his head, and he ran excitedly after it. 'It's just right!' he shouted. Clare found a sheltered spot and sat on a blanket while her husband and son attempted to fly the kite. Raine ran vigorously down the hill, the small red shape of the kite spiralling along the grass behind him, refusing to fly. Thomas followed. Clare smiled as she watched Raine and Thomas run in a line across the down for the fifth time. She was facing the setting sun. Sunlight glinted off the canal and the railway tracks. The prison jutted out like a red bolt. 'I wonder what it's like,' she said to Raine, 'knowing you've only hours to live, that you're going to be strangled.'

'Don't think about it,' Raine said, as if to himself. He left his wife and son and for half an hour walked alone along the ridgeway. He passed through a thin copse of silver birch trees, stepping over puddles the colour of milk. Shadows of clouds darkened the bare flesh of the plain. He thought of an insect crawling across a discarded green garment. This image of a despised thing crawling over a discarded thing to which it had no connection, and from which it would be flicked away, was like despair.

The next morning, Carver refused breakfast. At the prison, a large crowd had gathered. A constable had to clear a way through for them. It was cool and dark inside the building. They went into the room where Molina was being prepared. Carver waited by the door while a priest intoned the last rites. Molina started to speak rapidly in Spanish. Carver took out an old watch from his breast pocket and brought it close to his eyes.

'Where's the interpreter?' Raine asked the governor.

'Yes, it was very unfortunate,' the governor said in a whisper. 'Last night when we asked the prisoner whether he wanted the priest to attend on him today he became agitated. The interpreter, Mr Rodriguez, broke down and stormed from the prison. It seems that the prisoner, to gain Rodriguez's support, renounced his religion months ago. Rodriguez has a hatred of the catholic church. This is what my chaps tell me.'

'Does the priest understand Spanish?'

'No.'

'We must find another interpreter. The prisoner must be allowed to make his confession to a priest who understands him.'

'I've tried. There's no one else.'

The priest, an old man, was becoming confused and irritated by his failure to calm the prisoner. Carver walked over to the governor. 'It's almost time,' he said. 'If I may be permitted to take over?'

'Yes, go ahead Mr Carver.'

'But this is insufferable,' Raine said.

'The execution must go ahead at the allotted time,' the governor said.

Carver took hold of the young man by the shoulders and hoisted him to his feet. He gave him a flask and watched as he drank its contents greedily. 'Blood of Christ,' Carver said softly. 'Good boy.' He knew that the sight of the crowd would restore Molina's dignity. The crowd never failed to have this effect on a condemned man or woman. It was a law of behaviour confirmed by Carver in countless experiments over forty years. Molina became calm and the warders were able to escort him from the room.

They crossed the prison yard in a procession, watched by a face at every barred window. The gates were opened, and Molina followed Carver up the ladder and onto the high platform with its view of the crowd and the fields beyond. The old priest had been left behind, but Molina was calm. Raine watched from a distance as Carver tied Molina's legs together. The hood and noose were placed over his head, the trap door crashed open, and he dropped. A gasp then a silence; a creaking of the rope as the body turned clockwise, then anti-clockwise, then clockwise again. He had dropped, Raine calculated, no more than five feet. Five minutes elapsed before Carver cut him down. Molina's body was thrown into a plain wooden coffin and carried back into the prison.

The crowd dispersed. Raine noticed Hunt, the murder victim's husband, standing alone, still looking at the gallows. He was dressed in an old brown suit and was holding a bowler hat in his hands. Raine went up to him, but it was hard to know what to say. 'It's over,' Raine managed at length.

'He didn't deserve that,' Hunt mumbled.

The remark worried Raine, and as he thought about its meaning a detail in the constable's report started to peck at his brain. When he arrived home, he went into the kitchen and asked his cook, 'How long do potatoes take to cook on the stove?'

'About twenty-five minutes, sir.'

If Molina had killed Mrs Hunt, it must have been before twelve. Hunt was expected home for lunch at one. She would not have put the potatoes on to cook over an hour before lunch. On his next free day, he went to the village and spoke to the constable. 'Of course I'm sure. Potatoes were cooking on the stove. What of it?'

The following Sunday Raine returned to the village and waited for Hunt outside the church. He watched as Hunt, moving awkwardly in his best clothes, shook hands with the vicar and walked away from the others. He crossed the graveyard, his fingers at his throat to loosen the stiff collar. In his other hand, he was carrying a small bunch of flowers which at that moment he stooped to place on his wife's grave.

Raine had only questioned Hunt once. He had spoken to him in the village pub on the day of the murder. And he remembered that the vicar and Hunt's employer had arrived. His interrogation of Hunt had been cut short and subsequently, with the capture of the Spaniard, there had been no need to speak to him.

Raine caught up with Hunt at the door of his cottage. 'I've been waiting for someone to come,' Hunt said. 'You better come in.'

Raine followed Hunt into the kitchen. 'Shall we sit here?' Raine asked, indicating the table.

'If you like. I need a drink.'

Hunt fetched a bottle of gin and two glasses.

'I don't drink, Mr Hunt, but you go ahead.'

Hunt poured and drank four glasses of the spirit without pause. 'Will they hang me?' he asked. 'But why should I care, I deserve no less.'

'Tell me what happened, Mr Hunt.'

Hunt told Raine how he had come home early and discovered his wife with the Spaniard. 'He was going at her like a dog, here, across this table, my wife, Mr Raine, like a dog. Instead of confronting them, I went to the pub like a coward. I returned home at one. My wife was preparing the lunch, all smiles.' Hunt paused.

'What did you do, Mr Hunt?'

'I hit her. She mocked me. I picked up a knife and stabbed her.'

Raine felt sick with failure. 'How did Molina get the coat?'

'He must've taken it.'

'Will you sign a statement?'

He nodded.

Raine started to write a simplified account of Hunt's confession. A shotgun was leaning against the wall near the door. Hunt had been contemplating it for some time. Raine noticed, but he kept writing. He pushed the paper across the table. 'It's as you told it. Just sign your name at the bottom.'

Hunt signed his name. 'Will you let me go outside for a few minutes?'

'Yes.'

Hunt stood, took the shotgun, and left the

cottage. Raine went to the window and watched Hunt cross the meadow, the gun resting on his shoulder. The sun was setting. Light fell across the meadow and sparked against the barrel. Hunt entered the wood.

Raine let it happen. A shot rang out. Birds rose like shrapnel from the treetops. He followed Hunt's path across the meadow and into the darkness of the wood. Hunt's corpse was slumped against a tree trunk red with blood. Half his head was missing. Raine went back to the cottage. Hunt's confession was resting on the table. Raine was an honest man, but he knew that if he told the Chief Constable he would be blamed and ordered to stay silent. He found some matches in a drawer and set light to the paper. He dropped it in the sink and watched it burn.

Notes

'Cease to Weep' is a re-edit of an unpublished novel written in the early 1990s.

'The Portrait' is a re-edit of an unpublished novella written in 2001. It was inspired by Jean-Jacques David's *Portrait of Juliette Récamier* and Guilaume Guilon-Lethière's *Portrait of a Girl with Portfolio*.

'The Encore' was first published in *Shenandoah* literary magazine in 2014 (vol.64, n.1).

'The Last Public Hanging' forms part of an unpublished novel called *Necessity*. It was written in the 1980s.